How many *Fairy Animals* books have you collected?

 Chloe the Kitten

Bella the Bunny

 Paddy the Puppy

Mia the Mouse

 Hailey the Hedgehog

Sophie the Squirrel

 Poppy the Pony

 Daisy the Deer

And there are lots more magical adventures coming very soon!

Fairy Animals

of Misty Wood

Daisy the Deer

Lily Small

EGMONT

With special thanks to Susannah Leigh.

EGMONT
We bring stories to life

Daisy the Deer first published in Great Britain 2014
by Egmont UK Limited
The Yellow Building, 1 Nicholas Road, London W11 4AN

Text copyright © 2014 Hothouse Fiction Ltd
Illustrations copyright © 2014 Kirsteen Harris Jones
All rights reserved

The moral rights of the illustrator have been asserted

ISBN 978 1 4052 6871 4

1 3 5 7 9 10 8 6 4 2

www.egmont.co.uk

www.hothousefiction.com

www.fairyanimals.com

A CIP catalogue record for this title is available from the British Library

Printed and bound in Great Britain by The CPI Group

56330/1

MIX
Paper
FSC FSC® C018306

EGMONT LUCKY COIN

Our story began over a century ago, when seventeen-year-old
Egmont Harald Petersen found a coin in the street.

He was on his way to buy a flyswatter, a small hand-operated
printing machine that he then set up in his tiny apartment.

The coin brought him such good luck that today Egmont has
offices in over 30 countries around the world. And that lucky
coin is still kept at the company's head offices in Denmark.

Contents

CHAPTER ONE

Sweet Dreams, Misty Wood

It had been a beautiful day in Misty Wood, and now the sun was ready to go to sleep. As the sky turned from bright blue to deepest

purple, the stars began to twinkle and the moon climbed to join them. Down below, the Bud Bunnies were curled up in their cosy burrows, the Pollen Puppies' tails had stopped wagging, and the Cobweb Kittens snoozed in their mossy beds.

But not *everyone* was asleep.
Oh, no. Some fairy animals were
just waking up! They were sniffing
the cool evening air, fluttering their
wings and thinking about their
special jobs that made Misty Wood
such a wonderful place to live.

On the banks of Moonshine
Pond, the Moonbeam Moles
had already popped out of their
tunnels and were bustling about
gathering their nets. Soon, they'd
all be busy collecting moonbeams
to drop into the pond so that it
would glisten and shine.

Over on Sundown Hill, a
Dream Deer called Daisy was
stretching her long slender legs.
She blinked her big brown eyes,

smoothed her pale blue fur and
flexed her silvery wings. Daisy's
special job was to fly around
the wood at night, delivering
wonderful dreams to the sleeping
fairy animals.

'I think I have the best job
of *all*!' Daisy sighed happily. She
bounded to the top of Sundown
Hill and gazed down at Misty
Wood. Usually it was very quiet
at night, but tonight the wind

was rushing around, making the grass whisper and the trees rustle. Leaves whirled this way and that. But Daisy didn't mind. She spread her wings and the breeze caught them, lifting her into the air.

'Wheeeeee!' she cried as a gust blew her down towards Golden Meadow. 'It's going to be fun, flying in the wind tonight!'

She landed lightly at the edge of Golden Meadow, where the

flowers ended and the trees began.

'Time to start work!' she said.
She trotted slowly along a little
pathway that snaked between
the trees, looking out for any
sleeping fairy animals. It wasn't
long before she caught sight of
some little white whiskers and cute
pointy ears, tucked into a cosy
nook in a tree trunk.

'I know those ears,' Daisy
whispered with a smile.

They belonged to Connie the Cobweb Kitten, one of Daisy's friends. Connie was fast asleep. Daisy tiptoed closer, then poked her soft nose into Connie's snug, warm home. The little kitten would receive Daisy's first dream of the night!

'You've just left Dewdrop Spring, where you collected a big basket of dewdrops,' whispered Daisy in the kitten's velvety ear.

'There are enough to hang on *all* the cobwebs in Misty Wood, to make them sparkle and shine! And then you see a big bowl of fresh cream.'

Connie's button-nose twitched

in her sleep, and she gave a tiny, happy meow.

'It looks delicious,' Daisy went on, 'but you're not sure if it's for you. Then you see a name on the bowl – *CONNIE*. It *is* for you!'

Connie licked her lips with her little pink tongue and she began to purr. Daisy smiled and crept away, knowing that Connie would enjoy her bowl of cream for the whole night.

11

Daisy leaped elegantly into the air and let the wind carry her towards Moonshine Pond. Above the water, the Moonbeam Moles flitted to and fro, catching moonbeams in their nets. Daisy couldn't be sure, but they looked as though they were working doubly hard tonight.

She spotted a pretty mole with rich purple fur and silver-grey wings.

'Yoo-hoo, Maddy!' she called, cantering along the bank.

Maddy was Daisy's best friend. Sometimes, when they'd both finished their work for the night, they would go off together to play in the meadows. It was lovely to share the moonlight with a friend when all the other animals were asleep.

Maddy swooped and landed next to Daisy, waving her net.

13

'Hello, Daisy!' she said, sounding a bit out of breath. 'I'm really sorry but I can't stop and chat tonight.'

Daisy glanced up at all the moles whipping to and fro in the wind. 'Why, what's going on? You all look so busy.'

'Yes,' said Maddy, her dark eyes shining. 'We're having a competition. And you'll never guess what – the first prize is a

yummy pudding. A big bramble-
berry crumble!'

'Ooooh,' Daisy gasped, her
mouth watering. 'Bramble-berry
crumble's my favourite!'

Maddy smiled. 'Mine too!'

'So, what do you have to
do for your competition?' asked
Daisy.

'The first mole to collect
one hundred moonbeams wins,'
Maddy explained.

'One hundred? That's loads!'
Daisy exclaimed. 'Do you think
you can do it?'

Maddy peered into her net.
'I'm doing *quite* well,' she said.

'I've already got about twenty. I'd better keep going because I really, really want to win.'

'Yes, of course.' Daisy nodded. 'I'll come back to see you later. Good luck!'

Daisy watched as Maddy took off, whizzing after a moonbeam with her net. She soon caught it, and Daisy grinned. Maddy stood a good chance of winning – she was so determined.

All the same, Daisy felt glad she
didn't have such an energetic
job to do. Hers was much more
peaceful. She opened her wings
and flew off towards Heather
Hill, where she was sure she'd
find plenty of sleeping animals to
whisper dreams to.

At the foot of the hill stood
some old oak trees. Their twisting
roots made lots of nooks and
crannies that were perfect for fairy

animals to sleep in. As Daisy drew
closer, she spotted a small bundle
curled up on some leaves. She
floated down to see who it might be.

'A Hedgerow Hedgehog!' she
exclaimed to herself as she landed
beside him. 'Now, I wonder what
sort of dream he'd like?'

She thought for a moment,
then bent down to whisper in the
little hedgehog's ear. But just
as she was about to begin, he

jumped up, his prickles spiking
out in all directions. Daisy leaped
back quickly, before a spike hurt
her nose. The hedgehog started
running round in circles, flapping
his russety-red wings.

'Hey,' Daisy called. 'I thought
you were asleep!'

The hedgehog stopped
running and looked up at her with
sad, fearful eyes. 'No,' he said.
'I wasn't. I'm awake.'

20

'I can see that,' said Daisy. 'But you're a hedgehog, and hedgehogs aren't supposed to stay up all night! You must be so tired from tidying up leaves all day. I was just about to give you a lovely dream.'

The hedgehog's bottom lip began to quiver. 'I don't want a dream,' he said in a wobbly voice.

Daisy stared at him. 'But everyone *loves* dreams.'

21

DAISY THE DEER

The hedgehog shook his head. 'Well, I don't. And I don't want to sleep.' He stamped his tiny foot. 'In fact, I'm never going to sleep. Never, ever, EVER again!'

CHAPTER TWO

The Hedgehog Gobbler

'Never?' Daisy's big brown eyes opened wide.

'No, never!' the hedgehog cried. He curled up in a ball and

24

began to sob. 'And you can't make me!' came his muffled voice.

'It's OK,' Daisy said softly. 'Don't worry. I won't try to make you sleep. But will you tell me your name?'

'I'm H-H-Herbie,' the hedgehog stammered.

'Hello, Herbie. I'm Daisy.' She sat down beside him. 'So, why don't you want to sleep?'

A fat tear rolled down Herbie's

cheek. 'Because of the Hedgehog Gobbler.'

Daisy stared at him in astonishment. 'The . . . what?'

'The Hedgehog Gobbler!' cried Herbie. 'He's a horrible monster that comes and gobbles up hedgehogs while they sleep! He creeps up from behind and then he opens his big mouth with its rows of jaggedy teeth and . . . *chomp*! He gobbles you up.'

Daisy frowned. 'I've never heard of a Hedgehog Gobbler before.'

'Well, he's around here somewhere,' Herbie said, peering over his shoulder. 'He could

pounce at any time. That's why
I'm going to stay awake forever
from now on. I'm never going to
go to sleep and let him catch me!'

Daisy tried to remember
all the different creatures that
she knew lived in Misty Wood.
There were Moss Mice and Bud
Bunnies and Petal Ponies and
Pollen Puppies. Cobweb Kittens,
Moonbeam Moles and Stardust
Squirrels . . . but she had never,

ever heard of a Hedgehog Gobbler.

'I really don't believe there's such a thing as a Hedgehog Gobbler,' she told Herbie in a gentle voice. 'I think you should try to get to sleep, and then I'll give you a lovely dream that will help you forget all about it.'

'But there *is*!' Herbie insisted. 'So I *can't* sleep!' His bright eyes filled with tears again.

'All right, Herbie,' Daisy said

hurriedly. 'But you're going to get awfully tired.'

The hedgehog wiped away his tears with his tiny pink paw. 'I won't get tired.' He fluttered his wings and flew in a circle. 'I'm wide awake – see?'

Daisy sighed. She could see that Herbie had made his mind up. But perhaps if he got *really* tired, he'd have to fall sleep. And she could definitely help him there . . .

'Well, I have an idea,' she told him. 'If you're going to stay awake, how about you help me with my job?'

'What, delivering dreams?' Herbie asked, looking a bit more cheerful.

'That's right,' said Daisy. 'If you come with me, you'll have to fly around all night, so the Hedgehog Gobbler won't be able to get you at all.'

Herbie started to grin. 'Wow. I'd love to,' he said. 'I think you have a brilliant job!'

'Well, yes, I do like it,' Daisy smiled. 'Come on then. Let's head for Honeydew Meadow first.'

They took off in a whirl of leaves. Herbie whooped with glee and chased after them. Daisy was pleased. The more energy the little hedgehog used up, the better. They dipped and dived, riding the breeze

THE HEDGEHOG GOBBLER

and enjoying the feel of the wind buffeting them to and fro.

When they reached the meadow, Daisy pointed down at a moss cushion surrounded with flowers, their buds shut tight for the night. On top of the cushion lay a Pollen Puppy, sound asleep.

'We'll start here,' she told Herbie as they landed next to the puppy.

'So, what do we do?' Herbie

asked, his eyes shining with excitement.

'We'll think of all the things that a Pollen Puppy loves,' she explained. 'Then we'll whisper them into his ear.'

'Ooooh. Well, I know they love juicy bones to chew,' Herbie said eagerly. 'And they love chasing each others' tails and scampering around the meadows flicking pollen and having fun.'

Daisy nodded. 'That's great, thank you,' she said. 'Now I can make a lovely dream for him.'

She bent forward and began to murmur into the puppy's floppy ear. 'You're having a wonderful time chasing your best friend's tail in Honeydew Meadow . . .' she began.

The Pollen Puppy's paws twitched, and his tail thumped against his mossy cushion.

'Look at him!' squeaked Herbie. 'He's really enjoying it!'

Daisy smiled, and carried on. 'You're bounding past a horse chestnut tree when all of a sudden you spot a delicious bone . . .'

The puppy gave a happy whine, and his ears pricked up in his sleep.

'The bone is big and juicy so there's plenty for you to share,' Daisy whispered. 'You and your

friend have a lovely time, eating it
and playing with it together!'

The puppy rolled over on to
his back and wriggled in delight,
his paws waving in the air. Daisy
stepped back, proud of their work.

'That was fantastic!' Herbie exclaimed as they slipped away. 'Can we do another one?'

Daisy grinned at him. 'Of course!' she said. 'Come on, let's go into the Heart of Misty Wood. Lots of fairy animals will be asleep in there.'

They glided towards the centre of the wood, then swooped down between the trees and began to flutter along nearer the ground,

watching for sleeping creatures.
Herbie was clearly enjoying every
minute, but he seemed to be
getting sleepy, too. His flying was
getting slower and he gave a great
big yawn. Daisy slowed down,
feeling pleased. Her plan was
working! Soon Herbie would be so
tired he'd have to stop for a rest.
Then, when he'd dropped off, she'd
give him the best dream ever.

But suddenly Herbie cried out.

'Daisy!' he shouted. 'Stop!
Stop! It's the Hedgehog Gobbler!'

'What? Where?' Daisy whirled
round in a circle.

'THERE!' Herbie pointed
behind her with a trembling paw.

Daisy turned and gasped.

Right ahead was an enormous towering figure. It was making an awful groaning sound – and it had HUGE waving arms!

CHAPTER THREE

The Night Fright

Daisy gulped. 'Hide behind me,' she said to Herbie, sounding a lot braver than she felt.

Herbie didn't need to be told

twice. He scuttled behind Daisy.

Daisy took a deep breath and faced the figure. 'Who are you?' she demanded.

'I told you who it is. It's the Hedgehog Gobbler!' squealed Herbie.

Daisy tried to stay calm. *There's no such thing as a Hedgehog Gobbler*, she told herself firmly. Plucking up her courage, she took a step toward the huge creature.

'Careful, Daisy!' whimpered Herbie. 'I know you're a deer but it might get you, too!'

'Don't you worry, Herbie,' Daisy told him. She peered forwards to get a better look . . . then she sighed with relief. 'It's not the Hedgehog Gobbler,' she said, looking down at Herbie.

'It's not?' Herbie whispered.

Daisy smiled. 'No. It isn't a monster at all. It's a tree!'

'What do you mean, a tree?'
Herbie huffed, sticking out his
prickles. 'It can't be. It's got arms!'

'There's nothing here to
hurt you,' Daisy assured him. 'I
promise. Come on. Come and see.'

Herbie peeped round Daisy's
legs. Sure enough, all that stood
before them was a big old beech
tree. Its trunk was shadowy in
the moonlight. The 'arms' were
its branches waving wildly in the

46

THE NIGHT FRIGHT

wind, and the groaning sound was just its roots creaking.

Herbie's prickles began to calm down. 'Oh, yes,' he said happily. 'Silly me. It *is* just a tree.'

He scampered forwards and skipped all the way round the trunk, clapping his wings together as he went. Daisy sighed. At least Herbie felt safe again, for now – but the trouble was, being frightened by the tree had really

livened him up. Now he didn't look
the least bit sleepy.

'Let's go somewhere else,
Herbie,' Daisy suggested. 'I think
the trees look a bit too scary in the
moonlight. We'll go to Hawthorn
Hedgerows instead.'

'Good idea,' said Herbie,
fluttering along next to her. 'Lots
of Moss Mice sleep there.'

'Will you help me find one?'
Daisy asked.

49

Herbie puffed out his chest proudly. 'Of course.'

Sure enough, it didn't take Herbie very long to find a tiny Moss Mouse curled up in a cosy nest of twigs and moss.

'Well done,' said Daisy. 'You're being a big help. Now, let's think. What do Moss Mice like?'

'Poppy seeds,' Herbie said at once. 'And hawthorn berries. I think they like *my* favourite food

50

too – yummy hazelnuts. And they love being all together, having fun with their families and friends.'

Daisy nodded. 'Thank you. That's plenty to work with.' She bent down to make a perfect dream for the mouse.

'It's your birthday,' Daisy whispered into his tiny ear.

The mouse's nose and whiskers twitched in excitement.

'All your friends are here,

and your whole family too,' Daisy
continued. 'Everyone's having a
lovely time. Your mum has made a
delicious hawthorn-berry pie, and
there's hazelnut cake for afters.'

'Yum!' Herbie exclaimed, rubbing his tummy. 'Make sure they all sing a song,' he added. 'I love it when fairy animals sing songs at parties.'

Daisy smiled and nodded. 'Everyone eats piles of poppy seed pancakes,' she whispered to the mouse. 'Then they all sing "Happy Birthday" to you. It's your best birthday party ever!'

They watched as the mouse

53

gave a little squeak of happiness in his sleep, and then they tiptoed away. Another good job done!

Daisy led Herbie to Dandelion Dell, where the flower-heads were closed up for the night. The stems were rocking to and fro in the breeze. 'Are you tired yet?' she asked the little hedgehog. She was quite sure that he must be by now.

'Not a bit,' said Herbie. 'I'm getting hungry though.

And thirsty.' He looked at Daisy hopefully. 'Where do you think we should go next?'

Daisy sighed. However was she going to get Herbie to sleep?

'Let's go to Moonshine Pond,' she said. 'You can have a drink there. And maybe we'll find a snack on the way.'

As they started flapping their wings, a big gust of wind whisked them both up into the air. Herbie

did a loop-the-loop as the breeze
lifted him.

'Wa-*heyyyyy*!' he yelled as he
zoomed past Daisy, upside-down.

Daisy dived after him,
laughing, then chased him all the
way across the meadows and dells.
As they swung round a clump of
bushes, she spotted something
dangling in the moonlight.

'Herbie!' she called. 'Come
back here!'

Herbie did a somersault in the air to turn round.

'You said you were hungry, didn't you?' asked Daisy.

'Yes, I'm starving!' Herbie said, zooming up.

'And I think you said that you love hazelnuts?'

'Ooooh yes,' Herbie cried. 'They're my favourite. Why, have you found some?'

'A whole bush of them,' said

57

Daisy. 'And they're just ripe!'

Quickly, they gathered a
little pile of the nuts and Daisy
helped Herbie crack them open
with a stamp of her hoof. Herbie
chomped his way through half of
them, and then stopped.

'I'm full now,' he sighed,
rubbing his tummy. 'But I could
really do with a drink.'

'No problem,' Daisy said,
launching herself into the air

again. 'We're not far from the pond now.'

Above Moonshine Pond, the Moonbeam Moles were still hard at work, gathering moonbeams as fast as they could. While Herbie

swooped down to the banks of the
pond to slurp the crystal-clear
water, Daisy looked around for her
friend Maddy. She flew over the
pond, weaving in and out of all the
busy moles, but there was no sign
of her.

'That's strange,' muttered
Daisy. 'Wherever has Maddy got
to? Surely she's still here catching
moonbeams?'

And then, just as Herbie flew

up to join her again, she spotted Maddy – all alone on the banks of the pond, standing by a clump of bullrushes.

'There's my friend,' she told Herbie. 'Let's go and talk to her!'

As they fluttered down to land beside Maddy, Daisy's heart gave a little thud. She could tell at once that something was wrong. Maddy was looking very gloomy. Her silver-grey wings were drooping

and her velvety fur looked flat.

'Maddy, what's wrong?' asked Daisy.

Maddy gave a loud sniff. 'There's been a disaster,' she said in a trembly voice. 'A *total* disaster, in fact!'

CHAPTER FOUR

The Lost Moonbeams

'A disaster!' Daisy exclaimed.

'What's happened?' Then she

noticed something was missing.

'Maddy, where's your net?'

'That's the disaster,' said

Maddy, a tear trickling down her nose. 'I was just chasing a lovely big moonbeam when the wind came along and blew my net away – *whoooosh!*'

'Oh, no!' Daisy felt so sorry for her friend. Maddy had been working really hard.

'It was nearly full, too.' Maddy sat down and buried her face in her paws.

'But that's not so bad, is it?'

65

Herbie asked, looking puzzled.

'Can't you get another net?'

Maddy gave a little sob.

'Yes, but – but not tonight. Not

in time to win the competition.'

She quickly explained the rules

to Herbie. 'And I was so close! I almost had a hundred moonbeams and now they're all lost!' A tear rolled down her face and she wiped it way with her paw.

'Oh, Maddy, please don't cry. We'll help you look for it,' Daisy said kindly. 'It can't have gone too far. Herbie here will help, won't you, Herbie?'

'Of course I will.' Herbie gave a little skip of excitement. 'I love

hunting for things. Hide and seek
is my favourite game ever.'

Maddy peeped at them from
between her paws. She was looking
a teeny bit hopeful now. 'Would
you?' she asked.

'Yes! Come on, let's go – there's
no time to lose!' cried Daisy.

Herbie was already up in the
air with his wings spread, riding
circles on the wind. 'Let's look in
trees first!' he yelled.

He shot off at full speed with Daisy and Maddy just behind. The branches of the trees were swinging to and fro, their leaves jostling and rustling, but there was no sign of Maddy's net. So they flew on towards some small bushes on the other side of Moonshine Pond. Herbie dived under them, and whizzed over them but there was still no sign of the net.

'Now where can we look?'

DAISY THE DEER

wailed Maddy. 'I'll never find it. And I'll never win the bramble-berry crumble!'

But then Herbie glanced up. 'What's that?' he cried, his prickles on end. He looked at Daisy, his eyes wide with fear. 'Is it – is it – the Hedgehog Gobbler?'

Daisy followed his gaze and gasped. There was something very strange among the stars! A mysterious glowing light,

travelling quickly across the sky.

'No, no, no, that's not the Hedgehog Gobbler,' she reassured him.

'Yes it is,' Herbie said, flying round in fright. 'Those are his big scary eyes, glowing at us.'

'I told you, there's no such thing as the Hedgehog Gobbler,' Daisy said firmly. 'Shall we go and see what it really is?'

'Only if you go first,' Herbie

said fearfully.

'OK, come on then!' Daisy called. She launched off with Maddy and Herbie on her tail.

Up, up, up they flew, over the trees and high above the Heart of Misty Wood. The glowing object was still ahead of them, whirling and dancing in the wind. Daisy beat her wings even harder, until finally she got close enough to see what it was. And when she did, she

couldn't believe her eyes!

'Maddy, it's your net!' she called. 'It's glowing because it's so full of moonbeams!'

Daisy rushed after it, but Maddy and Herbie were struggling to keep up. Their little wings were whirring and they were out of puff already!

'Please – can – you – catch it – Daisy,' Maddy gasped. 'Your wings – are bigger – than ours.'

'I'll do my best!' Daisy cried.

She surged forwards after the net. The wind whipped through her pale blue fur and made her brown eyes water, but she tucked her head down and flew faster, faster, faster – faster than she'd ever flown before! Maddy's net spun and twisted through the air, turning cartwheels as it shot over the dark trees of the wood. Daisy swished this way and that,

75

DAISY THE DEER

THE LOST MOONBEAMS

following the net as it flew above
the treetops and headed towards
Dewdrop Spring.

Daisy beat her wings even
faster. Now she was close enough
to see all the different moonbeams,
glistening inside the net. She
hoped none of them had fallen out.

'One more push!' she said to
herself.

Closer . . . closer . . . closer!
She reached out with her long

neck, trying to catch the net between her teeth. But just as she was about to catch it, the wind snatched it and sent it spiralling towards Dewdrop Spring.

'Oh, no! It mustn't land in the water!' Daisy cried. 'We'll never get the moonbeams back if it does.'

She dived down, swooping towards the surface of the spring. The wind suddenly dropped, and the net began to fall down . . .

down . . . down . . .

'I'm going to be too late!'
Daisy puffed.

She flapped her wings as
hard as she could and zoomed
after it. She wouldn't give up! As
she opened her mouth to grab
the net with her teeth, she heard
a big SPLASH. She'd got it! But
what was that splash? Had the
moonbeams fallen out?

CHAPTER FIVE

A Special Visitor

Daisy rose up away from
Dewdrop Spring and circled
around to find Maddy and Herbie,
who were just catching up.

'You did it!' Maddy cheered.

'Yes,' said Daisy, passing her the net. 'But I'm really sorry – I think I lost some of your moonbeams. I heard them splashing into the water.'

'No, no,' squealed Herbie. 'We saw it all. It wasn't the moonbeams that splashed into the water – it was your hoofs!'

Daisy felt her heart leap. She was so relieved!

'Thank you, thank you!'

Maddy squeaked, fluttering around Daisy. 'Now I'd better go and make up for lost time. Maybe I can still win the competition!'

'Yes, yes, go go go!' Daisy exclaimed. 'And good luck!'

As Maddy raced off, Daisy looked down. Her legs and hoofs were dripping with water, so she shook them one by one to dry them, then turned to Herbie.

'You *must* be tired by now,

Herbie,' she said. 'That was a lot of flying, wasn't it?'

Herbie's eyes were beginning to droop. He put one paw up to his mouth to hide a yawn. 'Yes it was. But I'm not tired.' He blinked, then tried to open his eyes wide. 'Not even a tiny bit.'

'Are you sure?' Daisy asked gently. 'Wouldn't you like to snuggle down to sleep?'

'No! I told you – I'm never

84

going to sleep again,' Herbie

insisted, hiding another yawn.

Daisy gave her fur one last

shake, and smiled. 'Oh, yes, you

did say that. Well, we'd better do

something else then. How about

we go back to Heather Hill?'

Herbie looked at her suspiciously. 'But that's where I usually go to sleep for the night,' he said. 'You're not going to make me go to bed, are you?'

'No, no, of course not,' Daisy said soothingly. 'I need to find some more fairy animals to deliver dreams to, that's all. You can help me do that.'

Herbie nodded. 'All right then.'

Daisy sniffed the cool air and fluttered her wings. It was her favourite time of night. The stars were twinkling merrily, and the moon was at its brightest. It was when she felt at her most lively – but she could see that poor Herbie was struggling. As they took off once more, his wings would only beat very slowly – so slowly that he could hardly stay in the air!

'It's not too far,' Daisy said.

'We'll fly back up past Golden
Meadow, and you can have a rest
every now and then if you want.'

'I . . . don't . . . need . . .
to . . . rest,' said Herbie, but even
his voice sounded slow.

Daisy felt so sorry for him. She wished he would believe that there was no such thing as a Hedgehog Gobbler, but he was much too frightened. What could she do?

They flew up the valley, past tall, waving poplar trees, gnarled old oaks and blossoming hedgerows. They were about halfway up when Daisy thought she heard a strange whooshing

89

sound. She glanced at Herbie.
Could it be his tired wings making
a funny noise?

But then Herbie heard it, too.
'What's that noise?' he demanded.
'Is it the Hedgehog Gobbler?'

The whooshing was getting
louder, and louder, and LOUDER!

'It is!' Herbie yelled. 'It really
is the Gobbler this time!'

Daisy didn't know what to
say. The whooshing sound was

definitely very strange and scary, and she didn't know *what* it could be. She gestured at Herbie to fly down to the ground.

'Here it comes!' shrieked Herbie, making Daisy jump.

They cowered as a huge creature flew towards them. It had massive dark wings and enormous eyes. Even Daisy was frightened this time – it definitely wasn't a tree, or a net of flying moonbeams!

DAISY THE DEER

'Who are you?' she called out
bravely.

The creature swooped past
them and landed on the branch
of a sycamore tree. 'I am the Wise
Wishing Owl,' it hooted. 'Whoooo
are yoooooou?'

Daisy and Herbie heaved a
sigh of relief. Then they looked
at each other in amazement. The
Wise Wishing Owl? She was the
oldest and wisest creature in all of

Misty Wood, and the fairy animals hardly ever saw her!

'I thought you were the Hedgehog Gobbler!' exclaimed Herbie. 'I'm so glad you're not.'

The Wise Wishing Owl ruffled her feathers. 'The Hedgehog what?' she hooted.

'The Hedgehog Gobbler,' said Herbie, fluttering up towards the beautiful owl. 'It's really big, even bigger than you, and ten times

scarier,' he explained breathlessly.
'It's got huge teeth and a
ginormous belly, and it comes out
at night to find hedgehogs who are
curled up fast asleep. And then it
gobbles them up whole!'

'Is that so?' the Wise Wishing
Owl said, gazing at him with her
big round eyes.

'Yes! Yes!' said Herbie. 'We've
been trying to escape from it all
night!'

'Oh, dear.' The Wise Wishing Owl looked at Herbie gravely. 'Tell me something, young hedgehog. I have lived in Misty Wood longer than any other creature, but I have never, ever heard of or seen a Hedgehog Gobbler. So how do you explain that?'

'I don't know.' Herbie frowned. 'But I do know that he's out there and that I mustn't ever go to sleep again.'

The Wise Wishing Owl gave

a soft chuckle. 'All right,' she said.

'Tell me something else. Who told

you about the Hedgehog Gobbler?'

'My big brother, Horace,' said

Herbie.

The Wise Wishing Owl nodded. 'I thought it might be someone like that. Now, does Horace ever play tricks on you?'

'Oh, yes,' said Herbie. 'We play tricks on each other all the time. He loves hiding my breakfast or jumping out at me from behind a tree, so then I pretend to be a spiny dragon to scare him or . . .' Suddenly, his eyes opened wide. 'Do you – do you think the story

about the Hedgehog Gobbler is
one of his tricks?'

The Wise Wishing Owl smiled
and nodded. 'Yes, from what I
know about big brothers, I think
it most certainly is. Now, what
do you think he'd say if he knew
you'd stayed up all night worrying
about it?'

Herbie's cheeks went pink.
'Oh! He'd really laugh.' He looked
at Daisy, then the owl, then back

to Daisy. 'He'd better not find out, had he?'

'That's right,' agreed the Wise Wishing Owl, winking at Daisy. Daisy smiled and nodded.

'In that case, I'd better get back to Heather Hill as fast as possible,' said Herbie. 'I've got a lot of sleeping to do!'

'Thank you, Wise Wishing Owl,' said Daisy. 'I'm so glad we've sorted out the mystery of the

Hedgehog Gobbler at last!'

She and Herbie waved goodbye to the beautiful owl and rose up into the starry sky. Herbie managed to find one last burst of energy, and he sailed along on the breeze singing to himself.

'There's no Hedgehog Gobbler,' he warbled. 'There's *nooo* Hedgehog Gobbler!'

Daisy chased after him, chuckling to herself, until Heather

101

Hill was in sight. They swooped down to the old oak tree – the very same tree that she had found Herbie beside at the beginning of the night.

Herbie landed among the roots and snuggled down. He curled into a ball, then looked up at Daisy with his eyelids drooping. 'Thank you, Daisy,' he said drowsily. 'You've been a really good friend to me tonight.'

102

'Oh, that's all right,' said Daisy. 'You've been a big help to me, too. Perhaps we could have another adventure together one day.'

But Herbie didn't reply.

He had tucked his nose between his paws, and he was already fast asleep!

CHAPTER SIX

The Best Dream Ever

Daisy smiled to herself. 'Now it's Herbie's turn for the best dream ever,' she murmured. 'Let's see . . .' Daisy thought of all the things she had learned about Herbie.

She leaned close to his tiny ear, and began. 'You're out in the woods with your friends,' she whispered. 'You're all having loads of fun doing your special job, collecting leaves with your prickles to make Misty Wood lovely and tidy. While you're working, you play hide and seek, and you hide so cleverly that no one can find you for ages!'

Daisy gazed down at Herbie

and saw a happy smile curling up the corners of his mouth.

'And then, tucked into your hiding place, you spot something really tasty,' she went on. 'It's a big pile of shiny brown hazelnuts. When your friends find you at last, you show them what you've found and you all decide to have a hazelnut party!'

Herbie gave a tiny squeak of excitement in his sleep.

'You very kindly share all of your hazelnuts with your friends and, to say thank you, they sing you a song. And then you all begin to dance.'

As Herbie wriggled happily in his sleep, Daisy fetched some leaves to cover him so that he was even cosier than before. Then she slipped away quietly into the night, leaving him to his lovely dream.

With the moon beginning to
dip down across the sky, she knew
she had no time to waste – she
wanted to go and see how Maddy
was getting on.

Daisy flew back down the valley towards Moonshine Pond. As she went, she realised that the wind had finally dropped, and the trees and hedgerows lay still and silent under the sparkling stars.

At least Maddy won't lose her net now, Daisy thought. *Maybe she'll have managed to catch her final moonbeams just in time.*

By the time she arrived at the pond, all the moles had

finished work for the night. They
were gathering on the banks by
the willow trees, holding their
moonbeam nets. The competition
must be over already! Daisy
rushed forward to see what was
happening. Where was Maddy?
And who had won?

And then she spotted her
friend. She was standing right at
the top of the bank by a fallen
tree trunk. Meredith, the oldest

Moonbeam Mole of Misty Wood, was standing on the trunk as if it were a stage – and she was making an announcement.

'And the winner of our special bramble-berry crumble competition is . . . Maddy!' she exclaimed. 'Maddy, please step forward to show everyone your net!'

Maddy looked as though she would burst with pride. She

hopped on to the tree trunk and waved her net, which was bulging with all her moonbeams.

'Well done, Maddy. You were the first mole to collect one hundred moonbeams,' Meredith said, smiling at her. 'And now here's your special prize.'

Daisy and all the moles clapped and cheered. Maddy bowed to everyone before accepting the delicious pudding.

DAISY THE DEER

The smell of the crumble wafted over to Daisy, and her mouth began to water. She was so happy for her friend.

'Now, I know that Maddy will be dying to taste her prize,' said Meredith. 'But first, there's an important job to do. We have all worked very, very hard tonight collecting our moonbeams. And now it's time to place them where they belong – in Moonshine Pond.

So, Maddy, as our winner, would you please lead the way?'

Maddy nodded eagerly. She put her crumble down on the tree-trunk stage to keep it safe, then she fluttered up and above the water with her net. She tilted the net and tipped out the moonbeams. They rippled gently into the water, lighting it up with a soft pearly glow. All of the other Moonbeam Moles did the same,

until Moonshine Pond glistened and shimmered more beautifully than Daisy had ever seen before in her life. It looked amazing!

'Well done, Maddy!' Daisy called out.

'Daisy!' Maddy exclaimed happily, trotting back up the bank. 'Come on – you have to help me eat my crumble!'

'Oh, no,' said Daisy. 'You won it – it's all yours!'

'Don't be silly,' Maddy said with a smile. 'If you hadn't caught my net for me, I never would have won. And anyway, there's far too much of it for just me.'

Daisy grinned. 'Well, if you're sure,' she said. 'Thank you!'

Together, they fetched the crumble and sat down by the trees to eat it. As Daisy took her first bite, she closed her eyes. It was the yummiest crumble ever.

'Mmmmmm,' she mumbled.

'Mmmm mmmm!' agreed Maddy.

Their mouths were too full to say anything else!

Daisy gazed over to the east, where the first hint of dawn was turning the sky from purple-black to deep blue. What a night of adventure it had been! As the crumble settled down into her tummy, she began to feel all warm and sleepy. She thought of Herbie enjoying his lovely dream, and smiled as she remembered how hard he'd tried to stay awake. Soon it would be bedtime for her

too, but she was quite sure that she
wouldn't have Herbie's problem.
Oh, no! She was so tired and
happy, it would only be seconds
before she was fast . . . asleep . . .

Turn the page for
lots of fun
Misty Wood
activities!

Help Daisy find Maddy's moonbeams!

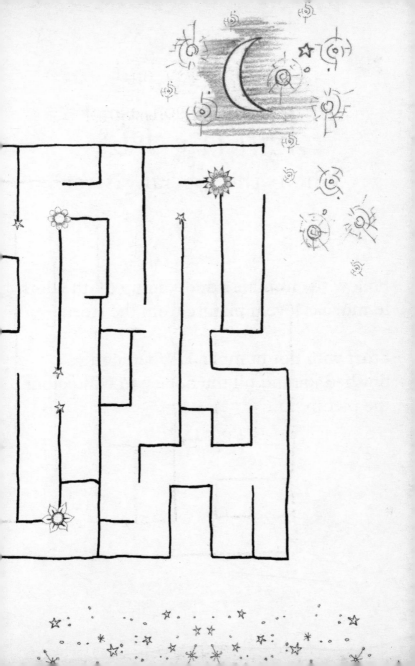

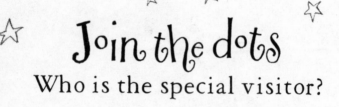

Join the dots

Who is the special visitor?

Follow the numbers and join up all the dots to make a lovely picture from the story.

Start with dot number 1. When you've finished joining all the dots, you can colour the picture in!

Draw a special dream for Daisy

Daisy's special job is to give dreams to the sleeping fairy animals of Misty Wood.

But can you give Daisy a special dream while she is sleeping?

EGMONT PRESS: ETHICAL PUBLISHING

Egmont Press is about turning writers into successful authors and children into passionate readers – producing books that enrich and entertain. As a responsible children's publisher, we go even further, considering the world in which our consumers are growing up.

Safety First
Naturally, all of our books meet legal safety requirements. But we go further than this; every book with play value is tested to the highest standards – if it fails, it's back to the drawing-board.

Made Fairly
We are working to ensure that the workers involved in our supply chain – the people that make our books – are treated with fairness and respect.

Responsible Forestry
We are committed to ensuring all our papers come from environmentally and socially responsible forest sources.

**For more information, please visit our website at
www.egmont.co.uk/ethical**